Giant the Lion

The Lion Who Could Swim

Written by Artemisa Gutierrez Laurence

Illustrated by Izzy Bean

"This book is dedicated to my family and friends who love and support me in all that I do. It is in gratitude that I share this book with you. A special thank you to my loving husband and son, who make all my dreams come true."

AGL

There once was a lion cub called Giant, and all he ever wanted was to swim. One day, he walked past the pond and saw his friends laughing and splashing in the water. He stood at the edge of the pond peering in longingly.

"Just dive in," said Flighty Mighty the Bird.

"I can't," said Giant. "I don't know how to swim." Giant looked down at his paws sadly.

"That's all right. We'll teach you," said Hara the Hippo.

The word spread and soon more friends came to encourage Giant the Lion. Amongst the crowd, there was Mother Duck and her baby ducklings, young Sally the Giraffe, Hara the Hippo, Flighty Mighty the Bird, Myrtle the Turtle, Fred the Frog, Todd the Otter, Betty the Butterfly and Al the Alligator. Everyone was anxious to show Giant how to swim.

"Just hop in," crowed Fred the Frog. "No, just creep in," bellowed Al the Alligator.

"Just stick your head in," said Sally the Giraffe. "Just blow bubbles," said Hara the Hippo.

With so much commotion from everyone yelling directions at him,

Giant became overwhelmed and didn't know where to start.

Myrtle the Turtle, the pond lifeguard, blew her whistle.

"Slow down," said Myrtle.

"We must show him one at a time."

"I'll start," said Mother Duck. She waded in with her three little ducklings in tow.

"Just waddle in like this." Mother Duck proudly swam to the middle of the pond. Little Giant gently dipped his paw in. He placed one paw in front of the other until he was standing in the water. The water was cold, but he was so happy to be there that he didn't care.

"Yay! I made it!" exclaimed Giant.

"Now, move your flippers," instructed Mother Duck as she moved her legs back and forth, swishing in a circle through the water.

"But I don't have flippers," said Giant.

"Well, just, move your paws," explained Mother Duck "Back and forth. You can do it," said Mother Duck with her sweet encouragement.

Giant moved his two hind legs around and front paws in a circle.

He was wading through the water!

"That's it!" cheered the ducklings.

"Wow, this is fun!" said Giant.

"Now stick your head in," cooed Sally the Giraffe.

"You mean get my face wet?" asked Giant, his eyes growing wide.
Sally giggled.

"Yes, silly," she said from the edge of the pond.
Giant shook his head.

"Do I have to?"

"How will you ever swim if you don't put
your head under water?" asked Sally.

Hara the Hippo crept up beside him and said,
"I'll show you. Let's blow bubbles! Put your lips together and blow air into the water."
Giant put his lips to the water and gently blew, and soon a few bubbles popped up.
"That's it," said Hara. "Now blow through your nose."
Giant blew through his nose, and bubbles started forming on top of the water.
It felt funny at first, but he liked it. He was blowing bubbles!
"Make sure to open your eyes,"
said Hara, so he did.

Giant dove under water to see all the beautiful pond life. Giant saw fish and tadpoles swimming. He came back up for air and saw everyone smiling at him.

"I'm swimming!" he yelled. His friends cheered.

Everyone was so proud of Giant.

"See, we knew you could do it!" said Myrtle.

Every day from then on, Giant swam circles around Hara. He practiced leaps with Fred the Frog, and he raced with Mother Duck's ducklings.
At the end of the day, he relaxed in the sand at the edge of the pond.

One day at the pond, Flighty Mighty flew onto
Hara's back and said,

"Hey everyone, listen up. I just came from
the bird council meeting, and I have exciting news.
The Bass Lakes Games is coming to our village!"
Everyone cheered.

"We must enter!" yelled Myrtle.

"Who will swim?" asked Hara.

"Well, Giant of course. Everyone
knows he's the fastest swimmer
now," said Myrtle.

Giant looked up in surprise.

"I'm not ready to swim in the Bass Lake Games," Giant said bashfully.

"Of course you are!" said Mother Duck.

"But I just learned how to swim. This is all new to me," said Giant.

"Yes, but you are a great swimmer! Remember how afraid you were to learn?" asked Mother Duck. Giant remembered back.

Yes, he had been scared to try.

"Do you think that it was easy learning how to leap? Do you know how many times I missed the lily pad?" croaked Fred the Frog.

"Do you think it's easy being tall? It took me a long time to learn how to gallop with speed," declared Sally the Giraffe.

"Do you think it's easy learning to fly? Do you know how many times I fell down?" asked Flighty Mighty the Bird.

"We taught you how to swim, and now you outswim all of us. You have a dedication to swimming," Myrtle said. Giant nodded.

"Well, I do love swimming. And it did become easier the more I practiced."

"I'll be your coach!" cried Myrtle. Everyone snickered.

"Why are you the coach?" asked Al the Alligator.

"Just because I'm slow on land, doesn't mean that I am slow in the water," huffed Myrtle. "I could swim circles around all of you!" said Myrtle. More snickers from the group.

"I'll show you," said Myrtle, and she dove right in and zipped around each one of them. Their jaws dropped in awe, amazed at how fast she was.

"Okay, you can be his coach," agreed Al sheepishly.

"I'll work with Giant on his breathing," offered Hara. "He needs to know when to come up for air if he's going to swim fast.

'One, two, three and breathe," Hara instructed.

"Breathe every third stroke and look on both sides if you want to see your competition."

Mother Duck raised her wing. "I'll work on his freestyle.
Arms must go straight up in the air and land in front, pushing away the water gracefully."

"And I'll work on his backstroke," added Todd the Otter. "Lie on your back,
tummy high up in the air. Arms go straight up and reach back by your ears.
Then you reach back and pull the water, " said Todd.

Fred the Frog hopped forward.

"I'll work on his frog stroke, which is also known as breast stroke. Front paws form a small circle and push down, while the back legs do a frog kick," said Fred. Betty the Butterfly fluttered in front of them. "I'll work on his butterfly stroke! Do two double kicks, come up for air, and spread your arms like a butterfly spreads her wings," said Betty the Butterfly, demonstrating with her pretty wings.

"But what will I do?" asked Myrtle the Turtle. "I'm his coach, you know!"

"You'll do what coaches do best," said Mother Duck. "You'll train him to excel with your great motivational skills. You have a way with words."

"Why, yes I do," said Myrtle.

Everyone was willing to train Giant and to cheer him on.

"Okay, everyone. We have three months to train," said Myrtle. "We must start today. Flighty, go tell the bird council that Giant the Lion will be representing Shell Pond."

Every day Giant went to the pond and Hara the Hippo trained him on his breathing. Mother Duck worked with him on his kicks. Sally the Giraffe concentrated on his underwater breathing. Fred the Frog helped him practice his start dives, and Al the Alligator worked on his flip turns and speed.
Mother Duck's three ducklings huddled in a corner practicing their cheers.

"Giant the Lion, swaying through the water. Hear him roar, and he will soar!"
This made Giant very happy.

Giant was faithful in his training practice, but soon became so exhausted that he couldn't swim anymore. Every stroke became difficult and tiring. One day Giant said,
    "This is hard. I don't want to do this anymore."

"You can't give up cub. You have talent," said Flighty Mighty.

"You're right, swimming is my talent and I am good at it!" exclaimed Giant. Everyone raised their paws and wings in celebration.

"Just keep practicing and visualize yourself winning," said Myrtle the Turtle.

"Okay, coach, I'll do my best," said Giant.

The day of the Bass Lake Games finally arrived and herds of animals from all around the world gathered to watch the games.
The birds' sports media crews were there to report the events.
The World Swimming Animal Council speculated who would win the gold medals in the competitive sport of swimming.

As Giant the Lion entered the arena with his coaches, Team Alligator sneered as he passed by.

"Ha! Who are you?" asked Wally the Alligator from Team Alligator.

"I'm Giant the Lion," said Giant. Team Alligator all laughed at him.

"Giant? You are nothing but a cub! You're too small to be called a Giant." They all laughed.

"I'm not too small, and I can swim! Just you watch." declared Giant.

"Who's your coach, the turtle?"
laughed Wally and his Team
Alligator crew. Myrtle the Turtle
rose in front of Giant and responded,
    "Well, as a matter of fact, I am.
And it's Coach Myrtle to you!" said Myrtle,
sticking her nose in the air.
Team Alligator laughed at the thought
of the small turtle training
little Giant.

"This is my team of coaches," said Giant the Lion proudly, standing in front of Myrtle the Turtle, Hara the Hippo, Mother Duck, Sally the Giraffe, Fred the Frog, Todd the Otter, Betty the Butterfly, Al the Alligator and Flighty Mighty the Bird.

"Your team of coaches?" Wally the Alligator laughed even harder.

"And who is that frog? Is he your 'leap' coach?" asked Wally as his teammates roared with laughter.

"Never mind them. They apparently don't know good manners nor good sportsmanship," squawked Mother Duck.

"Yeah, mama, you tell them!" said Dolly the Duckling.

"It's 'yes,' girls. Now, carry on," she told her ducklings.

"Yes, mother." said Dolly the Duckling. They waddled along as little Dolly looked back, huffing and raising her tail.

It was time for the 100-yard sprint, when Giant would compete.
The bird sports media crews were on the sidelines ready for the race to begin.
Dolly and her sisters cheered,
    "We don't know what you've been told, but we have come here for the gold!"

The bird announcer bellowed into the microphone.

"Now calling for the 100-yard sprint, which will consist of four laps of the lake," he said.
The crowd cheered.

"In lane number one, we have Wally from Team Alligator of Alligatia. This is Wally's third time at the Bass Lake Games. In past games, Wally has won two bronze medals.

"In lane number two, we have Charles of Team Crocodiles from the country of Croc. This is Charles' fourth Bass Lake Games, and he earned a silver medal in last year's games. He is going for his first gold medal this year.

"In lane number three, we have newcomer Giant the Lion. Giant is a lion cub who recently learned how to swim and was trained by a team of coaches from his pond. He's here to represent Shell Pond, and this is his first Bass Lake Games."

"In lane number four, Frances is here to represent her home country of Hippolatia."

The crowd roared with excitement as the announcer finished listing all the names of the competitors. Off went the start whistle and the race began. Wally was off to a lead start after diving long head first in the water. Giant dove in and did the flutter kick like Mother Duck showed him.

Giant was swimming with his arm strokes, high in the air, and he breathed every third stroke like Hara taught him.
Charles the Crocodile swam with long strides and moved in front of Giant and bypassed Wally the Alligator.

They all swam close to each other, almost neck and neck with each lap and each flip turn. Then Charles the Crocodile swiftly took the lead ahead of Wally and Giant.

Charles won the race, earning him gold.
Wally the Alligator finished in close second, winning the silver.
Giant the Lion finished in third place, winning the bronze.

After the medal ceremony, Wally and Charles raced over to Giant.

"Hey cub, sorry we were so rude to you. You swam great out there! You were so fast, you had me nervous," said Wally. "You swam quite gracefully. Where did you learn how to swim like that?" asked the charming Charles.

"My team of coaches taught me," Giant said as he looked over at his coaches who were beaming at him.

"Well, they did a great job," complimented Wally.

"Yes, we made a great team," said Giant proudly as he raised his cub fist in pride at his friends.

"Well done," said Mother Duck flapping her wings.
"Bravo!" croaked Freddy the Frog hopping in glee.
"But I came in third place and won the bronze," Giant reminded them.
"Well, what's wrong with bronze?" asked his coach, Myrtle the Turtle.
"I wanted to win," said Giant.

"You didn't give up. That's what winning is," added Myrtle the Turtle. You kept trying until you succeeded. And you succeeded big today.

"We're all so proud of you," said Mother Duck. Giant smiled and was happy to have his team of coaches to support him.

"It's like how you all used your talents to teach me how to swim," said Giant. They all had done their part.

"How does that saying go? 'It takes a village to raise a cub?'" said Mother Duck.

"I'll say!" said Coach Myrtle.

As they prepared to leave, Dolly the Duckling and her sisters were still cheering.

"Oh, girls, where do you come up with those cheers?" asked Mother Duck.

"It's our gift, our talent, mama," said little Dolly.

"Yes, that's true," smiled Mother Duck at her ducklings.

And Giant and his team of coaches began to return to Shell Pond with their bronze medal where it all began.

Swimming Safety

Never swim alone.
Always swim with parental / adult supervision
and lifeguard on deck.
Always swim with a friend.
No diving off shallow end.
No running around the swimming pool.
No rough play and no pushing.
Wear a life jacket when you go boating.
No glass in pool area.

About the Author

Artemisa Gutierrez Laurence is an educator who holds a Master of Arts in Education, and has taught children how to swim as a Water Safety instructor for over 25 years.

"After teaching children how to swim for many years, I discovered that many children are fearful to learn. However, once they learned how to breathe, kick,and swim, children were surprised at how well they did. They soon realized their strength, skill and love of swimming. Like anything else you want to achieve in life, you just have to try and you may just discover your gift and talent to share with the world."

About the Illustrator

Izzy Bean is a freelance children's book illustrator from Yorkshire, UK

After graduating from the University of Bolton, Greater Manchester, in 2006, with a degree in Illustration and Animation, Izzy has honed her skills to provide bold, colourful and expressive illustrations in a recognisable style. When she isn't illustrating, Izzy likes to read, take long walks amongst wildlife and spend time with family.

Made in the USA
Las Vegas, NV
23 March 2022

46178064R10029